13

SO-BTA-526

Crystal Kingdom Adventures

adapted by Emily Sollinger
based on the screenplay by Chris Gifford
illustrated by Victoria Miller

Ready-to-Read

Simon Spotlight/Nickelodeon
New York   London   Toronto   Sydney

Based on the TV series *Dora the Explorer*® as seen on Nick Jr.®

SIMON SPOTLIGHT
An imprint of Simon & Schuster Children's Publishing Division
1230 Avenue of the Americas, New York, New York 10020
© 2009 Viacom International Inc. NICK JR., *Dora the Explorer*, and all related titles, logos, and
characters are registered trademarks of Viacom International Inc.
All rights reserved, including the right of reproduction in whole or in part in any form.
SIMON SPOTLIGHT, READY-TO-READ, and colophon are registered trademarks of
Simon & Schuster, Inc.
For information about special discounts for bulk purchases, please contact Simon & Schuster
Special Sales at 1-866-506-1949 or business@simonandschuster.com.
Manufactured in the United States of America
First Edition
2 4 6 8 10 9 7 5 3 1
Cataloging-in-Publication Data is available for this title
from the Library of Congress.
ISBN 978-1-4169-8498-6

Hi! I am .

DORA

This is my 📕 .

BOOK

My 📕 has lots of stories.

BOOK

Do you want to read a story

with 🐵 and me?

BOOTS

Once upon a time there was a .

CRYSTAL KINGDOM

There were four CRYSTALS

that filled the with

CRYSTAL KINGDOM

colors.

The made the shine.

YELLOW CRYSTAL   SUN

The made the .

BLUE CRYSTAL   SKY   BLUE

The made the .

GREEN CRYSTAL   TREES   GREEN

The made the shine.

RED CRYSTAL   RAINBOW

A greedy KING

lived in the .
CRYSTAL KINGDOM

He did not like to share.

He hid the .

CRYSTALS

After that there was no more

color in the .

CRYSTAL KINGDOM

The people were sad.

A girl named worked

ALLIE

hard to look for the .

CRYSTALS

She looked

behind .

ROCKS

She looked

behind .

FLOWERS

She looked and looked.

"Look, Dora! is jumping

ALLIE

out of your ," says .

BOOK   BOOTS

"I am looking for some

missing ," says .

CRYSTALS   ALLIE

 can help us find the !

MAP   CRYSTALS

says the is in the

YELLOW CRYSTAL

 story and the is in the

DRAGON

GREEN CRYSTAL

is in the story.

CAVE

The is in the

BLUE CRYSTAL

magic story.

CASTLE

The is in the
RED CRYSTAL

story.

CRYSTAL KINGDOM

We have to jump into the
BOOK

o find all of the .
CRYSTALS

Come along!

The knows where the

DRAGON

 is.

YELLOW CRYSTAL

"The hid it in the

KING ROCKS

on the , " says the .

CLIFF DRAGON

"I will take you there."

The breathes

DRAGON   FIRE

on the 🪨 to free the ◇ .

ROCKS   YELLOW CRYSTAL

Yay! We got the ◇ .

YELLOW CRYSTAL

Our next stop is the .
CAVE

A friendly says
BUTTERFLY

the is inside a .
GREEN CRYSTAL   COCOON

"Look!" says .

ALLIE

"The are hatching!"

COCOONS

There is the !

GREEN CRYSTAL

The has a surprise for us.

BUTTERFLY

She gives us all !

WINGS

The is in

BLUE CRYSTAL

the magic .

CASTLE

But the greedy

KING

locked the !

CASTLE

How can we get inside?

I can use my
WINGS

to fly through the .
WINDOW

We found the !

BLUE CRYSTAL

We have to find the .

RED CRYSTAL

"The hid the

KING   RED CRYSTAL

in his ," says .

CROWN   ALLIE

"But he is on top

of that big ."

VOLCANO

How can we get to
the top of the ?
VOLCANO

We can use our
WINGS

to fly there!

The KING tries to stop us.

Mine, mine, mine!" he says.

Share, share, share!" we say.

He gives us the !
RED CRYSTAL

Now we have all the ! CRYSTALS

The colors are coming back!

The and are !
SKY · SEA · BLUE

The ☀ is ✦!
SUN · YELLOW

The and 🌳 are !
GRASS · TREES · GREEN

The 🌈 is shining!
RAINBOW

We saved the !

CRYSTAL KINGDOM

We even got the greedy

 to share.

.NG

He gives his to and

CROWN   ALLIE

nakes her the !

QUEEN

We did it!

Hooray!

Thanks for helping us

find the !
CRYSTALS